T0274491

WAR PRIMER

THE GERMAN LIST

ALEXANDER KLUGE

WAR
PRIMER

TRANSLATED BY ALEXANDER BOOTH

Seagull
BOOKS

LONDON NEW YORK CALCUTTA

This publication has been supported by
a grant from the Goethe-Institut India.

Seagull Books, 2024

Originally published as *Kriegsfibel 2023*
© Suhrkamp Verlag Berlin, 2023
All rights reserved by and controlled through Suhrkamp Verlag Berlin

First published in English translation by Seagull Books, 2024
English translation © Alexander Booth, 2024

ISBN 978 1 80309 395 6

British Library Cataloguing-in-Publication Data
A catalogue record for this book is available from the British Library

Typeset by Seagull Books, Calcutta, India
Printed and bound by Hyam Enterprises, Calcutta, India

'GIVEN
MEN AS THEY ARE
THE TREES SURRENDER'

Ben Lerner, *The Lichtenberg Figures*

CONTENTS

FIGURE 1. Lenin mourns.

STATION 1

'WAR IS BACK AGAIN'

FIGURE 2. [Translation: Children are the real chronologers of war.]

FIGURE 3

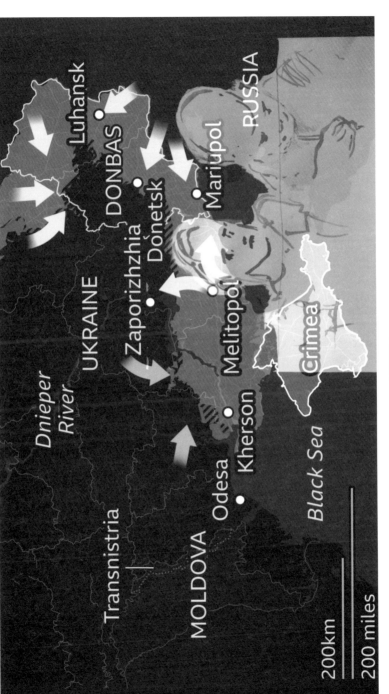

FIGURE 4

CONSIDERING A SMALL CHILD IN 1908

The curtains waved in the midday sun like sails full of wind. The windows of the children's room onto the garden were wide open.

The child was asleep, arms outside the blanket so as not to sweat. It passed gas a few times, digesting. The young mother was waiting for her husband to be home at one o'clock sharp. The enzymes of his stomach, his blood-sugar levels like clockwork; otherwise, a generous man. To avoid any disturbance of the punctual process, she had fed the child beforehand and now had time to wait.

The child took after the young woman's favourite brother. But what can be determined by unmistakable signs or memories of other family members in a creature that changes daily? She'd be able to distinguish this child's features from that of all the other children in the world, no matter how agitated or dirty or how diffuse the light. But she would not have been able to list the individual factors upon which that overall picture within her was based. The face of the sleeping child could not be compared with its face when it smiled or laughed throughout the day.

In 36 years, that creature would be as old as she was now. That would be in 1944. The waiting woman did not know that, when the alarms began to soun, in that distant year, young women would be rushing to the bunker at the zoo, a concrete building that far exceeded other stone monuments and that was successfully destroyed only three years after the war.

FIGURE 5. My mother Alice, born in 1908.

WE SCHOOLKIDS HAD NO IDEA ABOUT THE DANGER IN WHICH WE WERE FLOATING IN DECEMBER 1944

The degree of danger we students of the Cathedral Gymnasium of Halberstadt were facing in December 1944 wasn't in our heads at all. During breaks, we played 'fighter pilot'. Impersonating 'Spitfires' and 'Hurricanes'—British planes from the early phases of the war— we ran down the steep street past Westendorf secondary school, our gymnasium's substitute building. Back in our classrooms, we parsed sentences from Caesar's *Gallic War* into their individual grammatic parts. The way we were working here, and running around a quarter of an hour before, were not 'warlike'.

The word 'danger' differentiates itself from the words 'accident' and 'perish' by the degree of probability with which the designated event occurs. A 'danger zone' is not defined by something happening, but by a threat. In those 'heartgrey' December days full of 'snow as slush', there was nothing on our minds but our day-to-day lives as students.

During that winter of 1945, German tank units broke through the thin American lines in the Ardennes. I later learnt that this last 'massed motorized force' was to cross the Meuse River and advance on Antwerp. The Western Allies' supplies were to be cut off. The road maps for the troops, all the logistics, were based on papers from the blitzkrieg of 1940. At the time of the attack, the clouds were hanging low over the valleys of the Ardennes, and had the weather not improved over Christmas Day, the American air force might not have been able to stop the advance. WHICH COULD HAVE PROLONGED THE WAR IN EUROPE BY NINE MONTHS. The danger of which we students were unaware was that, in summer 1945, the ready-to-use atom bomb would not have been detonated in east Asia but in the middle of the German Reich. Papers from the Pentagon reveal that, had the war in central Europe not been over by August 1945, there were plans to bomb Ludwig-shafen. Alternative target: Lüneburg Heath. Mathematicians from Göttingen involved in the development of the bomb considered the latter a suitable place not only in terms of impact but in sparing the lives of US troops as well.

Until the failure of the Ardennes offensive, that is, for about ten days, 'OUR DESTINY' could have taken this direction and led to the use of just such a murderous wonder weapon. In a war, once a great power has decided on a particular plan it is difficult to reverse. It is not only when the lethal material is dropped: the arrow of time cannot be turned around even at the planning stage.

That kind of danger—although objectively present for a short time in the tangle of causalities—lay completely outside our powers of imagination as students.

PRACTICAL EXPERIENCE PLAYING WITH TIN SOLDIERS

A popular method in battles with tin soldiers is to REVERSE FIRE when under artillery attack. Such a reversal of the already spent ammunition surprises and confuses your adversary, in this case my classmate Alfred Müller, who later became an oral surgeon at Charité Hospital, Berlin. A battle of tin soldiers is most likely to be decided quickly by a so-called wonder weapon. In the meanwhile, however, we were busy re-enacting the 'Battle of Leuthen'.

'SPRING WITH WHITE FLAGS'

At 13, I was an observer of the last two months of the Second World War in my central German hometown. Since my birthday in February 1945, I had been 13 years old. But my experience and observational capabilities were those of a 12-year-old. That's how I became a witness. I was still several months away from the fate of being drafted into the ranks of the flak-helpers.

My hometown burnt in the firestorm. Following the air raid of Sunday, 8 April 1945. We students could reliably differentiate between the silver silhouettes of British and American bombers. The units I saw departing over us during our escape from our already burning but still intact home through Kaiserstraße's ravine of fire towards Braunschweiger Straße were American. I walked towards the school of the deaf, in the direction of Bindseil pool. The water there was supposed to protect my sister and I from the fires. I saw Karl Lindau, the muscular and powerful proletariat stoker of our home, hunkered down in a hole. We children, however, could already see the planes' wings as they flew away.

Three days later, on Wednesday, 11 April 1945, my small family—my father, my sister and I—were sitting on the edge of town at Domeyer nursery. Awaiting the arrival of the Americans on Braunschweiger Chaussee, to the right and left drainage ditches, alongside them trees, the main road in-between. In the early afternoon, a slowly moving column of tanks drew closer. To the left and right, a row of marching GIs. Positively reacting to the white flags raised in the nursery and in all the houses marking the road into town. From Burchardianger, a civilian, 1938-style cabriolet turned onto the main road. Its occupant: a high-ranking Nazi party member, was stopped by the US troops, searched for weapons, placed on the radiator of a jeep and driven to the rear of the column. Once they had passed, we children plundered the cabriolet which the GIs had tipped into the ditch to clear the road.

I can say with certainty (a 'memory gap' here is impossible): at no moment did I associate the troops with the planes that had destroyed the town three days earlier. There is no general term 'enemy' for the observational skills of a 13-year-old. The Reich borders of 1937 were not something that occupied my imagination or my senses. I was interested in maps, but those of distant countries, I was curious. Hours later, outfitted with handcarts, we stormed the commissariat, that massive brick building in which supplies for the German army had been stockpiled for the period until about autumn.

ONE ACCIDENT IN A MILLION

The trail coming under fire, a mother sent her three children off towards the forest, led by the eldest, an eight-year-old. She told them to walk to a woodpile they'd passed the day before and wait for her there. But the children didn't find the right one and wandered on through the forest, from one wood pile to the next. Soon they got lost and continued in the direction they thought would lead them home, to the place from which they had set out. Their mother looked for them in vain at the agreed meeting point and then further and further afield. She had already lost contact with the trail. No matter how far she walked, she found no trace of the children. Even after the war, her search was in vain. Where had the children gone? Had they starved to death? Had they run away to someone else? Had they disappeared?

'ONCE YOU'VE REACHED A CERTAIN POINT OF MISERY, IT DOESN'T MATTER WHO CAUSED IT. IT JUST HAS TO STOP.'

A statement of Frau Anna Wilde, my friend Fritz Wilde's mother, mother of six. Frau Wilde worked as a cleaning woman in various households. Her husband, a deadbeat. The day of the air raid, this industrious worker from Baden, with her own children and several children from the homes in which she cleaned, fled to the so-called GROTTOES in Spiegelberg Park, sandstone hollows considered bombproof. To this woman, there was no such thing as 'universal'. Regardless of which party of the Second World War had formu-lated it, no *casus belli* would have convinced her. She would not have fought for any 'values to be defended'. Having said that, she was ready to fight to the end for her children. She would have found the word 'Volksgemeinschaft' to be nothing but a word. During the time my hometown belonged to the German Democratic Republic, this woman succeeded in becoming the head-server of a canteen in a factory that produced marine pro-pellers. With an intricate system concerning the UNOFFICIAL EXCHANGE OF BLACK-MARKET GOODS BETWEEN LARGE ENTERPRISES, she laid the groundwork for that system which had supported her rise. Which is to say, she didn't do it for any sys-tem at all, but for her brood. A SMALL, THIN WOMAN. LIVELY AND POSSESSING INDOMITABLE MENTAL STRENGTH TO FIND UNEXPECTED WAYS OUT.

Spring with White Flags, film triptych. 1 min 27 sec.

Children are the Real Chronologers of War. 3 min 1 sec.

STATION 2

THE UTOPIA OF ARMOUR

FIGURE 6

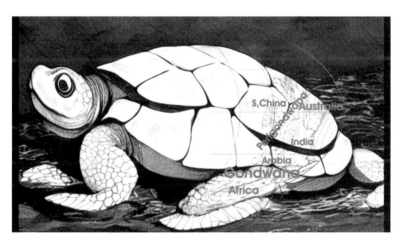

FIGURE 7

The Utopia of Armour. 5 min.

15

A CONVERSATION CONCERNING THE TURTLE, THE 'ARMOURED ANIMAL'

– Turtles are an ancient species.

– How soft their flesh is beneath the shell!

– Their shell made them immune to predators.

– Well, except for human beings, the gourmand who appreciates turtle soup.

– They are 'old world' animals. They come from a time more than 66 million years ago, long before the catastrophe that wiped out such a large part of earth's living creatures.

– That had nothing to do with their shells. Frogs with their elastic skin, consisting of nothing but soft parts without any so-called armour plating, survived too.

– Speaking of armour, does anyone have any idea why these animals survived while so many others did not?

– How should I know?

Both conversationalists were specialists at a laboratory in Silicon Valley researching substances that are to bring about longevity. Weighing as much as it does, neither of them believed armour to be a good solution.

UNDER THE SIGN OF MARS
CHARACTER-ARMOUR AND MOBILE WARFARE

Heiner Müller and I had travelled to the community centre of Garath, an area of Düsseldorf. We were there to support parliamentary deputy Jürgen Büssow in his electoral campaign. A day earlier, still in Berlin, Müller had burnt his hand and underarm while cooking on an open flame. After our appearance in the plenary, we sat down. I had brought along my film crew from Munich. It was customary for Müller to determine the topic of conversation. As an example, he remembered that in the Second World War, when tanks had their fuel and ammunition hit by anti-tank weapons, those inside were burnt alive. 'When tanks are hit, they become iron coffins.' When he started a conversation in such an associative way, I had to hold back with my questions. After a while he would shift his opening 'in a new direction'. This is what he referred to as 'spherical dramaturgy', taking his cue form one of Sergei Eisenstein's diary entries.

He quickly came to Shakespeare. He talked about the latter's *Coriolanus*. Coriolanus was a Roman aristocrat and general who had turned against the faction of the plebeians, a rebellious majority of his own people, and now, when the country was under threat from the enemy, remained passive on his estate, full of anger. Refusing to help. I ask Müller how he got to *Coriolanus* from tanks. 'Coriolanus,' he replied, 'is a tank.' His character is armoured. He has hardened his heart. And how does the play end? The play's climax, Müller said, is the soliloquy delivered by Coriolanus' mother. She breaks through the barrier he's erected about himself. In the end, Coriolanus saves Rome but loses his life as a result. It turns out that in the foggy days of April 1945, as a young flak-helper, armed with rocket-propelled grenades (the infamous *panzerfausts*), Müller and his unit had laid down in a ditch at the side of a road and watched 'Russian tanks go by like shadow machines'.

THE SEVEN SKINS (TANKS) OF
KNIGHT'S CROSS–RECIPIENT VON HÜNERSDORFF

A SCENE FROM THE YEAR-OF-THE-WAR 1943

On the first day of the battle of Kursk, a shell fragment had shattered his arm, that arm he had placed on the turret of his lead tank. Had the wounded man been brought to the troop area, he would have been saved. But he, poorly bandaged though he was, still wanted to punch through two defence lines of anti-tank guns. Headshot in the early afternoon. Crammed into the cabin of a Fieseler Storch (a small plane), his faithful companions manoeuvred the unconscious man to the field hospital in Kharkov. 'The shot-up face was unrecognizable to relatives.'

The head of the field hospital in Kharkov: this officer's wife. Specialists were flown in from Berlin. The commander-in-chief of the army group made hourly enquiries. After one week (and six emergency operations), Major General von Hünersdorff, the dream of his troops, was dead. All seven skins protecting him had proved to be deceptive. The skin (on his shoulders still, the signs of sunburn from early July, coated with cod-liver oil-ointment)—and this was in the nature of things—was not immune to bullets. A second skin was his confidence in the fortunes of war, the jaunty little field cap on his head, the aura of a man 'whom no bullet can hit'. This wasn't skin in the strict sense, but a special form of courage: the speed with which he changed positions. His tank was always in a different position from what the enemy thought. The third skin consisted of the vigilance of his comrades, they loved their idol and had shot him out of many a danger: shared courage, a cloud of motives. This cocoon was still intact at four o'clock in the morning when they started the engines.

Then the fourth skin: a new type of tank with concrete blocks on the metal, a protective bulkhead against enemy bullets that engineers had designed. But the newly built wall of reinvention deceived the occupants, in that the Russian artillery had a new type of high-speed ammunition, unknown of until that morning. It cut through the steel walls of the armoured skin as if they were 'made of sponge'. The innermost skin that protected him when all other skins failed was his confidence. It consisted—like jellyfish—of a body without a head: all interconnectedness. Such confidence is different from self-assurance. The weeks-long delay in attacking dictated by army command, the sweltering heat throughout the day, the nightly thunderstorms, in other words, the waiting, had ground down this confidence.

Another strong skin, like that of horny-skinned Siegfried, a kind of magic cowl, was the rumour that preceded Hünersdorff's armoured troops wherever he went and, up to then, had always confused the enemy: the terror, the anticipation of what would come with iron force as soon as his tanks appeared on the hill. In the battle of Kursk, on the very first day already, this protection was gone, without any of the fighters on either side realizing it. The final skin that could have saved von Hünersdorff was the military doctor's art. Just one year later (she learnt rapidly during the war), she would have been able to put together the Major General's splinter-riddled brain successfully and keep it—to a certain extent at least—functioning. Like AN ANGEL OF THIS SEVENTH SKIN, the young Frau von Hünersdorff stood at this candidate-for-death's head. And so, to sum up, a hero like this man possessed seven protective skins, all of which failed: first, the one about his heart; second, the one around his body; third, the one his troops provided; fourth, the iron skin of his tank; fifth, quick reaction skills (the antithesis of armour, these openly expose themselves to danger and escape it by not paying attention); sixth, long-distance action; seventh, *conduire amour* (never had the boss pushed the doctors of the field hospital anything like she did in the hour preceding her beloved's death).

HUMAN BEINGS ARE UNSUITED FOR THE ARMOURING OF THEIR HEARTS

The doctor Asclepios, Apollo's son—according to Ovid—generally advises against the armouring of the heart. An armoured heart might seem 'bulletproof' and hence of interest to a Stoic. And tyrants, too, deliberately seeking as they do to immunize themselves against any kind of empathy. The movements of this muscle, however, make it easy for doctors to determine that an 'armed heart' cannot beat. The armour is either too tight or too loose. Moreover, as far this son of God is concerned, it would be useless, as the heart would then be insulated from the skin and mind by iron or bronze. But if you took a softer material, a fabric, say, it wouldn't be armour.

GÖTTERDÄMMERUNG FOR AN ARMOURED FORCE

The Russian T-34 tank, progenitor of Russia's current heavy tanks, ran on diesel from Don to Berlin. They were considered difficult to conquer and stood in contrast to Western tanks: the descendants of race cars, these latter tanks ran on petrol and, though constructed in a much more refined manner compared to the T-34, were less solid.

The Iraq War and the most recent war between Azerbaijan and Armenia over Nagorno-Karabakh saw the Götterdämmerung come for Soviet weapons systems. Outfitted with Russian tank technology, the Armenian troops were helpless against Turkish and Israeli kamikaze drones.

ARMOUR'S LATEST UTOPIA:
MUTUAL ASSURED DESTRUCTION (MAD)

A drafter from the Institute of Strategic Studies sketched the deterrent as a kind of bell, a dome, beneath which, for example, the cities of USA would find themselves safe. The drawing served as a kind of lining for arguments in favour of a significant increase in the budget for the country's missile force. In the ensuing debate, however, the objection was raised that, in the end, this had nothing to do with any real kind of armour but simply a metaphysical one. This 'imaginary tank', the leading specialist of the congressional party opposing the increase stated, would only function in the adversary's mind. Should that particular mind fail to represent the drafter's bell to itself correctly, in other words, the danger, the armour wouldn't work. If, despite the threat, nuclear weapons were launched anyway, the only option would be to launch a counter-attack, that is, not to defend oneself but to avenge the act. Akin to a person slaughtered in battle seeking out their butcher the following night and killing them.

In fact, there is a myth of an Icelandic hero who, after battle (the one in which his deadly sword had raged), fell asleep with an extremely high blood-alcohol concentration and simply never woke up. His face, even in death, an angry red. This was subsequently credited to the young opponent he had slain the previous day, whose early death had pleased no one.

There is a memorandum to be found in the estate of a Russian admiral stating that, in the case of the Russian leadership being wiped out in a decapitation strike and Russian missil-launch facilities destroyed, the last submarine of a special class hidden in the depths of the ocean was to destroy USA's most important cities with a final series of nuclear missiles. But if awareness of this fact is not present at the right moment in the brain of the person who is to order the first strike, this is of no help to anyone. In the memorandum, the admiral discourages any kind of firm belief in MAD whatsoever.

WORDS AND THEIR OPPOSITES

War / Anti-war

Armouring / De-armouring

The armoured heart / No known opposite

The illusion of armour / Tank as burning coffin

Character-armour / Nature, empathy

STATION 3

CAUCASIAN AND UKRAINIAN STORIES / 'THE WONDER OF ANIMALS'

**GERMAN SOLDIERS
IN AUTUMN 1942
IN THE CAUCASUS.
IT IS 42.5 KILOMETRES
TO ELBRUS, THE HIGHEST PEAK**

FIGURE 8. The soldiers do not know why they need to fight here, so far away.

Making his way through France on a reading tour, officer and poet Ernst Jünger was transferred to Army Group A in the Caucasus. His Caucasian Diary *begins on 24 October 1942. As a privileged observer, namely, one with access to all the general staff and to the military leadership's secret plans, Jünger was a witness of the crisis affecting the German army at the eastern front. And that was the crisis which led to the encirclement of the Sixth Army in Stalingrad in November.*

A LONELY POETIC CHRONOLOGER
WITH A PRIVILEGED VIEW OF THE CRISIS
AFFECTING THE GERMAN ARMY IN DECEMBER 1942

In autumn 1942, the protectors of poet and captain Ernst Jünger, serving in Paris on the staff of the high commander in the West, thought it would be a good idea to send their protégé on a tour of duty to Army Group A in the Caucasus. The idea was to keep him out of the Nazi regime's interrogative hands. He was known to have carelessly made an appearance in circles of former Reichswehr officers who were opposed to the NATIONAL SOCIALIST REVOLUTION.

Far to the east, in the middle of the Caucasus Mountains, he was to give lectures and readings to the military staff. That seemed far enough away for Jünger's protectors, all high-ranking officers. The journey by plane and train—in stages—took weeks. Arriving in the area of operations, first in the foothills, then near the passes leading south over the Caucasus, he encountered an *actual world*, a frontline event that prompted him to pack up the 400-page manuscript he'd brought along—he'd imagined the trip would be something like a holiday and had intended to work on his manuscript, a 'thinking man's novel' concerning a lonely thinker's wanderings in Lüneburg Heath up by the North Sea—in wrapping paper and bind it together with rubber bands. What surrounded him there on the eastern front was serious: there was no space, no appropriate moment for a 'thinking man's novel'.

The words 'front' and 'war in the Caucasus' are, like 'eastern front', nothing but phrases, figures of speech. Their reality is experienced only when you are within striking distance of the enemy. Out there, there is no such thing as an overview. The senses scrabble, reason seeks but does not find the horizon.

The view from the command post of a higher-ranking centre of operations functions in a completely different manner. This view is directed onto freshly marked maps at a scale of 1:300:000. Seven to twelve times a day, but especially in the evening and at night, which is when the day's news arrived, Jünger followed the picture of an advance of the German eastern front that was in the process of failing. From Army Group A headquarters in the Caucasus events in neighbouring Army Group B a thousand kilometres to the north could be easily followed. This latter group commanded the Sixth Army, heading for encirclement at Stalingrad. The confusing reports did not provide the staff of Army Group B with anything like an overview. As they remained unaffected, however, those same reports were met with calm in the staff of Army Group A. And hence, Jünger noted in his *Caucasian Diary*, this SIDE LOGE provides you with a view of the THEATRE OF WAR that you don't get in any theatre anywhere.

Just three weeks later, the soon-to-become-legendary catastrophe was looming in the north between the Don and the Sixth Army in Stalingrad on the Volga. Jünger was the only poetic witness to record the nervous calls and fluctuating reports in his diary. The nights there in the Caucasus, following the encirclement of the Sixth Army in the cauldron of Stalingrad, were all rainy nights. Heavy, Black Sea rain. Half-awake, half-asleep, the poet had the impression that the mountain colossus, halfway up which the Russian and German fronts had frozen, was moving imperceptibly. The mountain range, a PIPE between the Caspian and the Black Seas, was moving imperceptibly, 'as if the earth were trying to shake off the foreign invaders'. But Jünger did not share this half-dream with his fellow officers in high places. He read from his *On the Marble Cliffs* instead.

Perhaps the poet was deceived by those images received in half-sleep: the MOUNTAINS, valleys and peaks were not moving particularly slowly. Rather, Jünger had the impression that, for many centuries, indeed for more than a thousand years, peoples, SWARMS OF YEARNING WALKERS, had been moving through the valleys and passes. But always on their way north from the south. Almost never in the direction in which two German tank armies and a mountain corps were now advancing from the north-west, pushing south. On the maps, it looked as if the arrows indicating vehicles and 'labourers in uniform' were moving over the mountain ridges through Georgia towards Persia. After dinner, officers of the intelligence department of the General Staff of the Army Group, Department 1C, had been telling Jünger about their plans to occupy the Arabian Peninsula 'abruptly'. They said—an excellent Burgundy was served—they had nothing at all in mind with the Caucasus. It was karst, rocky, slippery mud, and would soon be covered in ice and snow. But in the south the sun of Persia awaited.

An expert commission of petroleum engineers, drilling rig architects, pipe builders and transport specialists had already been accommodated in a collective building converted into a hotel in the conquered city of Stavropol. 'At the moment,' the lieutenant colonel who led the 1C branch said, 'they're still playing skat.' But in a few weeks' time—hopefully!—they'll be all action, building and constructing, and we'll be far below, heading for the Persian Gulf.

The poet, listening in his function as a POETICAL NOTARY, continued to have doubts about 'what exactly Europe wanted so far in the east'.

Jünger and some of the general staff officers working in the operations department, who were not guided by the huge blue arrows on the general staff maps—blue denoting the advances of the German troops—but by the counterattacks of the Russians marked in red, did not consider those weeks in November 1942 ideal for forging plans and nurturing hopes. 'We'd be better off,' they thought, but did not say, 'exploring and repairing the roads for retreat.'

FLARES IN THE EAST /
THE AUSTRO-HUNGARIAN MILITARY LINE
TO ASTRAKHAN

On 20 March 1918, officers of the Austro-Hungarian K.u.K. air force opened a flight route from Vienna to Lemberg (Lviv), Odessa to Kharkiv, Tiflis and Astrakhan.

The military administration had made a mistake. They had allowed private initiative into the middle of the war. The repair crews, the aviators' souls, the requisites for repairing aircraft were all concentrated on this new civilian line. Air fares for freight and passenger travel remained low. This particle, this Robinson Island of the peacetime economy, competed decisively with war capitalism. The private airline was fun. Eighteen pilots died. 'And if you don't use your life, you won't gain it' had to do with the fact that a group of officers and crews entrusted to them were there to conquer an eastern civil-aviation line for the postwar period, maybe even a new fatherland.

– At the end of an 'endless effort' is there always a continuation of the war by other means?

– Like 'flowers before you die'.

– So we'd have to look for entrepreneurial figures in the period around the end of the war in 1918 or 1945 (or at the end of the Gulf War) and revisit their perspectives in peacetime?

– There's a kind of moment of truth 'in the aftershock and the pre-shock of catastrophe'.

– Why didn't the Vienna–Lemberg–Odessa–Kharkiv–Tiflis–Astrakhan line ever become reality? Surely this revolutionary route through Europe triggers fantasies, right?

- Odd. There are records by Leshchenko, the tango king, that stretch along this very line. The 'plates' were pressed onto material from old Roentgen prints or X-rays ('ribs').

- That didn't affect the sound?

- On the contrary. These kinds of pressed ribs or plates—you just have to cut them round—preserve Leshchenko's immortal tango sounds forever and ever. Virtually indestructible material.

- Born out of necessity?

- There was nothing else.

FIGURES 9–12

WHY WASN'T IT POSSIBLE
TO MOVE AUSTRIA-HUNGARY
A THOUSAND KILOMETRES TO THE EAST IN 1918?

– Would the route from Vienna to Astrakhan have provided the Austro-Hungarian administration, which was experienced in governing a multi-ethnic state, the opportunity to rebuild in the already conquered east?

– Possibly.

– Could the route have provided the spark, as it did in Astrakhan?

– Plausible.

– Why didn't it work? Due to its being winter? The storms?

– No. The pilots rejected the company being saved by an American.

– Why?

– Arrogance. I don't think they recognized the quality of the bidder.

– So it wasn't on racist grounds?

– On unconsciously racist grounds. They didn't consider the bidder from New York distinguished enough.

– And yet had no reason to insist on such.

– No. But the bidder who would have taken over the airline was named Chaim Dryer and was originally from Lemberg, which he'd fled for New York.

– And the lieutenants and captains with military flying licences considered the man unsuitable to be their superior?

– Full of arrogance.

- What would have been the capital? Would there have been a chance of continuing?

- Without a doubt. The capital amounted to 500,000 dollars.

- The pilots thought they could keep the line going without any money but on the strength of the past?

- They wanted to keep it going on passion alone.

- Without passion, they would have taken a closer look at the offer?

- They definitely should have accepted it.

- And then there would have been a Budapest–Vienna–Lemberg–Odessa–Tiflis–Astrakhan (and maybe back in a circle over Smolensk) route?

- Together with the republics that can be founded along a flight line. A Central Europe. A continuation of the K.u.K. Monarchy to the East.

- Austria would have become a republic, a German-speaking one. The monarchy would have gone east with the help of planes?

- Together with the archdukes.

- And that would have been a valuable asset?

- Paid for by Chaim Dryer.

- And what drove him?

- Love for his homeland.

- Not capital interests?

- What harm do capital interests do to love of one's homeland?

REFUSAL TO SIGN A DICTATORIAL PEACE

This here is no peace treaty that I will ever sign. So spoke Leon Trotsky, the negotiator for the Russian delegation. What was presented to him in Brest-Litovsk was a dictatorial peace. The day before, to the surprise of the Soviet delegation, the so-called bread peace had been concluded between the German Reich, Austria-Hungary and the government of Ukraine. The Soviet delegation saw this as a snub. For the Russian side, continuing the war was out of the question, Trotsky continued. He refused to sign what was presented to him as a peace treaty. NO PEACE, NO WAR: DEPARTURE.

His own words had given this negotiator momentum. He considered his speech a success. No one in the stunned assembly answered him. As negotiations progressed, it became clear that the German side was unaffected by their apparent breakdown. On 18 February, nine days after the Russian delegation's departure, Germany's SUPREME ARMY COMMAND responded with 'Operation Faustschlag' (Fist Punch).

OPERATION FAUSTSCHLAG! TRAINS TRANSPORT SOLDIERS FROM WUPPERTAL AND HESSE, 'WESTERNERS', ALL THE WAY TO THE CAUCASUS

BLITZKRIEG ON RAILS

Colonel Hase, a member of the General Staff, referred to the course of 'Operation Faustschlag' as 'strange warfare'.

– We put a cannon, a machinegun nest and a group of infantrymen on railway wagons, drove to the next Russian-occupied station, arrested the Soviet personnel there, sent the prisoners to the rear with a second train and continued on to the next station with the cannon train.

– And the canon was where?

– On a flat wagon. In front of it, another flat wagon in case the train hit a mine.

– And the machineguns?

– One in front of the gun barrel, in other words, up front, the second on a wooden frame above the tender. The third at the end of the train. Flat wagon plus flat wagon plus locomotive plus tender plus Third Class passenger car plus final wagon.

CARE OF THE BODY

An 'expert' from Posen (Poznan) hurried on ahead of the German troops. In Tiflis, this licenced 'brothel owner' set up an establishment 'for the evening entertainment of officers from first lieutenant upwards'. Twelve young women were already on their way with the next transport. More special forces had to be recruited from the countryside. Suitcases full of costumes, as the 'erotic care of troops in a foreign country' is connected with quasi-theatrical performances, a piece of 'culture and entertainment'. The Rhineland-born expert conducts the first selection meeting of the newly recruited staff on the very day of their arrival.

THE FRONT EXPANDS EASTWARD
FAR BEYOND THE REACH
OF THE TELEGRAPH NETWORK

The news of 8 August 1918, on the BLACK DAY OF THE GERMAN ARMY IN THE WEST, reaches the Reich's outposts in the Caucasus by telegraph. TWO DAYS LATER. For the Bavarian cavalry squadron stationed in KABUL, on the other hand, news of the devastating defeat in the west took two weeks. There are no telegraphic lines over longer distances via PERSIA and AFGHANISTAN. It's a miracle that the news reaches the targets in the east at all.

FIGURE 13

FIGURE 14 AND 15. The soldiers do not know why they need to fight here, so far away.

UKRAINIAN STREET SCENES 2022

FIGURE 16

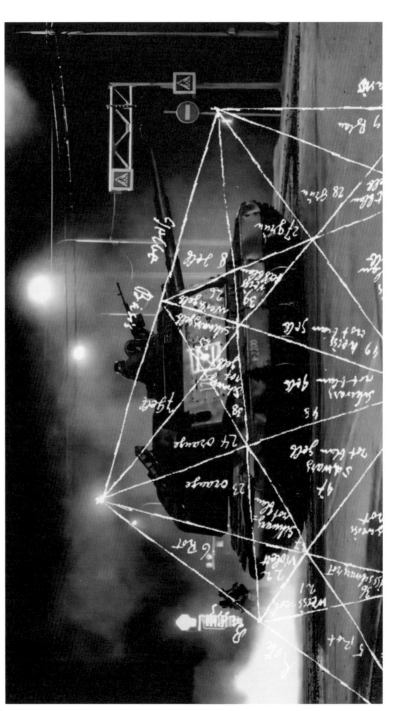

FIGURE 17

TWO SIDES TO A HAPPY ENDING

In the early days of the Ukrainian war, there was a report of a certain number of villagers, including young people and children, holding up a Russian tank. After a period of hesitation, the tank driver put it in reverse and rolled back out of the village.

This is an urban legend. It was already making the rounds during the Hungarian Uprising of 1956. During the 1991 coup in Moscow, the scene actually occurred several times and led to several tank divisions withdrawing from the city. In Beijing's Tiananmen Square, however, the same kind of confrontation ended in a massacre.

The report in the case of Ukraine emphasized the bravery of the civilians who opposed the tank. But it takes two to tango, as it were, for an encounter to end happily: the determination of the residents, but also that of the young tank driver, perhaps all of 18, who put the tank in reverse.

HOW NICE TO MEET 50 YEARS LATER, ALIVE, WHEN THINGS COULD HAVE TURNED OUT DIFFERENTLY

Sergei Gorbachev visited Bayreuth during his stay in Germany. After the Wagner opera had finished, he met the cartoonist Loriot. They sat together over a glass of wine. The conversation turned to Gorbachev, as a young boy of 11, observing German tanks in Stavropol (near the Caucasus) in 1942. With other youngsters, he had discussed whether they could be stopped. Loriot replied that he had been in Stavropol himself in 1942 as commander of a mechanized infantry company. A 'close encounter with danger'. A good feeling after 50 years that nothing happened.

Gorbachev and Loriot in Bayreuth. 8 min 19 sec.

FIGURE 18. Putin and Macron.

THE WONDER OF ANIMALS

Walter Benjamin's favourite children's book, *Bertuchs Bilderbuch für Kinder* from 1807—all 12 volumes of which Benjamin purchased again as an adult—features the depictions of ANIMALS.

They are pictures from a distant time, prints from the years when Caspar David Friedrich was working. Transposed into the current setting of the ATAVISTIC WAR in Ukraine, these animals are astonishing. Photography does not fully represent reality: Human desires are missing. 'If they are self-aware, they have animal shape.' (Derrida)

FIGURE 19

FIGURE 20. Film still from *The Wonder of Animals*: *The Mourning of the Creature*. Print on wood, 16.5 x 11 in. 2022.

The snake in Bertuch's 1807 *Bilderbuch für Kinder* clearly comes from a time and a lifeworld that is different from those in which 'a missile hits an apartment block in Ukraine'. The animal and the photographic image produce a contrast. This is an example of a 'time perspective'. You probably could not depict such a 'narrative perspective' through text alone.

The Wonder of the Animals: *The Mourning of the Creature.*
Film triptych. Featuring the funeral march from
Georg Philipp Telemann's opera *Emma und Eginhard.* 2 min 34 sec.

WHAT ARE BRICKS IN THE BUILDING OF A NATION?

Since the second Maidan, the Euromaidan of 2014, I have been working as an adult educator in the Republic of Ukraine. We teachers and journalists belong to the elite of our country, which has been independent since 1991. My job is to strengthen our country's identity in the hearts of our people. This includes narratively capturing the outline, vision and self-awareness, indeed the meaning, of our nation on a global scale. There is a lot of narrative art to catch up on. Training troops in modern weapons is easy compared to equipping them with a solid sense of national identity. The terrain of our state stretches over widely divergent territories, ones which have been historically unconnected for a long time.

The rivers criss-crossing the country from north to south carve up people's ability to visit one another, to be close. It would be better if our rivers traversed the country from west to east, connecting land areas like the Danube. Furthermore, at the end of the Second World War, the Soviet Union had gorged itself on former Romanian, Polish and pre-1914 Austro-Hungarian lands. Some of these 'imperial acquisitions' were never Russian, not even Ukrainian, and this diminishes the fabric of unity in the republic as a whole.

ONE OF UKRAINE'S GEOGRAPHICAL PARTICULARITIES THAT WE ADULT EDUCATORS SHOULD EMPHASIZE MORE

Twice a year the Black Sea rises. Every half a year, a piece of the sea's surface turns into a rainy cloud-bridge that flows violently northwards. This is the *rasputitsa*, six weeks in spring and six weeks in autumn. In a sense, a whole layer of the vast surface of the water rains down on the country, ensuring Ukraine's fertility, just as the Nile flood ensured the fertility of the Pharaohs' empire, Egypt, in ancient times.

When you count the months and days of sowing, harvesting, storing and being on standby in the hopes that fertility will return, you see that there is little time left for republic-building and creating public space—the agricultural areas of the community—except in the big cities. Between the GREAT WETNESS, the growing of the wheat and the harvest, there is an immense sequence of deadlines, of individual steps, for which time dictates a rapid beat. This is the law that we journalists and teachers, the farmers of 'second nature', also follow.

THE PHYSICS BEHIND 'SOLDIERLY RELIABILITY'

We're an American security firm. But not all of us are American citizens. You can rent us. But once the order has been placed, no power in the world could ever re-poach us. No client will shake us off. To get rid of us prematurely, we'd have to be shot. Once the job is done, however, we disappear from the face of the earth. None of us would ever betray the knowledge acquired over the course of a 'job' to a counter-organization. The knowledge is well stored in our chests. But I won't tell you what *chest* means. It is a piece of me that is detached from my head and my body. It has emigrated from the WEAKNESS OF THE HUMAN BEING. Were I to fall into the hands of an opposing organization and tortured, I wouldn't reveal a thing, for there is nothing of it in my soul, the one that feels pain. This knowledge is stored in my second soul.

The western secret service outfit I am currently working for in Ukraine recruited me on the Feast of St Nicholas 1989. As an agent and Dzerzhinsky-patriot of the GDR, I was smuggled onto the *Maxim Gorki*, a Soviet steamer. We were off the coast of Malta in a winter storm. The furniture in the salon where the negotiations were taking place moving back and forth across the floor. Many a porcelain object fell from the consoles and shattered. My job was to spy on our brother nation.

I was originally recruited by a company based in Cincinnati. The recruiter told me that they had been following my excellent work for months. A bean counter from the bankrupt mass of the imploding Eastern Bloc. I could just have easily been taken into the ranks of my comrades in the KGB. I would even have preferred that, as it would have suited my training better.

HOW DO YOU GET A HOME ADDRESS
AND TROOP UNITS WHEN INDIVIDUAL RUSSIANS
ARE INVOLVED IN LOOTING?

The soldiers in the Russian tank battalions are very young. In the evening, after a disappointing conclusion to battle, the leadership cannot stop them from looting. They lug furniture, carpets and valuables of all kinds into the trailers of their vehicles. Manage to pack the stuff into large, mailable parcels. Then the loot is tied up and transported to Belarus on trucks. From there, the goods are sent by post to the soldiers' homes. When we investigate such shipments, we learn the names, home addresses and places of recruitment, and thus the origin of the predatory units. Once we have the names of the perpetrators and their superiors, we feed our information cannons with what makes the news relevant in terms of *jus in bello*, that is, justifiable conduct in war: the precise attribution of offences, simultaneously to single offenders and to military units. As I've always said: information is a more effective explosive projectile than any artillery ammunition.

HOW MUCH WE MISS THE TEMPERAMENTS OF A GEORGE BUSH, SR., AND A PRESIDENT GORBACHEV IN 2022 /
MY IMPRESSIONS OF THE CREATION OF A SECURITY ARCHITECTURE ON 6 DECEMBER 1989 IN A WINTER STORM OFF THE COAST OF MALTA

On the Feast of St Nicholas 1989, US president George Bush, Sr., and leader of the Soviet Union, Mikhail Gorbachev, were aboard the *Maxim Gorki*, a Soviet steamer, to discuss EUROPE'S SECURITY STRUCTURE one last time. This meeting had come about thanks to the brisk changes overtaking the GDR. Desolate waters surrounded the ship. Certain rooms were flooded.

For eight hours that day, I was in fact a TRIPLE AGENT. I had been sent as a loyal advisor of the GDR ('of the people'). My comrades in the KGB (over whom I was watching) considered me one of their own. At the same time the moment I was recruited by our adversaries in the western services. The following day I was definitively a WESTERNER, and no longer in any kind of double role.

We security guards, mostly assigned as waiters, heard many a snippet of conversation from the proceedings, which were not conducted formally at set tables because of the ship's heavy rocking. There was a sense of unease. How easily a cadre of the National People's Army and a conspiratorial group of Russian officers in the Western Group of the Red Army could have got together in the vicinity of the capital of the GDR! Like what happened two years later in the putsch in Moscow. How little sabotage, diversion and use of armed force would have been needed that day to trigger a massacre like the one at Tiananmen Square! On historical days, which come as a surprise to everyone, there is no security in the world. Turbulence around the ship. And GENEROSITY in the lounges. The word 'courteous' has a slightly different meaning in

Russian, American English and German: three different 'masks of a word', but which, as a trio, denote an attitude in which one negotiator picks the other's brain and helps to avoid potential mistakes resulting from the speed of events. For a few hours, it didn't seem as if two opposing great powers were wrestling with each other but as if two builders were expertly repairing a house damaged by a hurricane.

HOW AMBASSADOR HOLBROOKE, SPECIAL ENVOY TO THE BALKANS DURING THE YUGOSLAV WARS AND SPECIAL REPRESENTATIVE FOR AFGHANISTAN, CAME BACK TO LIFE ONE MORE TIME

Over a nightcap at the Hotel Brussels bar following the conclusion of a NATO training conference, two intelligence pros, one English, one German, exchanged information concerning a negotiator at work in the east who their respective agencies had under surveillance. Apparently he was on a provisional research mission to explore possibilities for communication between Russia and Ukraine. Their notes referred to him by the code name 'the doctoral student': a 29-year-old man travelling back and forth between Alexandria, Tel Aviv and Istanbul. By ship and by plane. Supposedly paid by a foundation in the USA.

- His proposal for negotiation is absurd.

- Whose, the doctoral student's?

- Exactly.

- The chain of communication runs between a black marketeer in Alexandria, two oligarchs in London and their representatives in Istanbul, as well as a company in Tel Aviv. We're still investigating other contacts.

- One of the oligarchs is Ukrainian the other Russian?

- Yeah, and both of them are living in London. But they've got lobbying networks in their own countries. In the Russian's case, the walls of the Kremlin are porous.

The two agents, now ordering their second round, were proud of having been able to get wind of the so-called doctoral student's family background from out of all the gossip that attends to their line of work. The apparently savvy and ambitious 'contract-less negotiator' was of noble origins.

– They say that this young kid, who is obviously running at cross purposes here, is the illegitimate son of Ambassador Holbrooke. From a relationship with a Serbian woman.

– Is that certain?

– Maybe a legend because no one can figure it out?

– The affair with a Serbian woman right at the start of the Yugoslav Wars has been confirmed. The young kid grew up in the USA and went to Harvard.

THE *DOCTORAL STUDENT*'S SECRET 'TREATISE' IN WHICH HE COLLECTED HIS UNREALISTIC NEGOTIATION GOALS . . .

– You have a treatise here in your files?

– Yes, a passionate plea for the construction of a tunnel deep beneath the fronts of the war. Without all that much regard for realism.

– The young man is relying on one of Henry Kissinger's theories. Kissinger developed this particular one when describing the end of the Yom Kippur War.

– With a generous stroke of his pen, Egypt's President Sadat broke through the extremely detailed debate between the general staffs of Israel and Egypt concerning individual bunker lines, in sufficient numbers and positions, on both banks of the Suez Canal, thereby stunning Kissinger. In the middle of the Sinai Peninsula, a line is drawn that will permanently satisfies Israel's security interests.

– Solution to a 'tangle'.

When he was young, the German agent had attended training sessions run by the Stasi. He was one of the Federal Republic's rare acquisitions of a service member with a GDR background. Hence, he used the old-fashioned term DIALECTIC to describe the 'tangle' that preceded the conclusion of peace in the Yom Kippur War. His British colleague thought it was a word that needed untangling itself. At this 'joke', the two, who had become closer over the course of the evening, ordered their third nightcap.

WHAT DOES TANGLE MEAN?

– What did you mean by TANGLE before?

– A knot.

– You mean a kind of LOCKING-IN-PLACE?

– I mean something that, at the moment, seems insoluble. For either of the two sides. And whether one party wants to solve it and the other does not is irrelevant.

HEADING: TRIANGULAR RELATIONSHIP AS MODEL OF BALANCE' IN THE SO-CALLED TREATISE

The wiretap transcripts of the young man's contacts had to do with projects such as the reconstruction of Mariupol. To be financed by a billion-dollar fund made up of American, Russian and EU money. A NEW CASABLANCA. The reconstruction was to begin immediately, regardless of the bombings. But that is quite unrealistic, the British intelligence officer commented on the relevant passage in the treatise. 'Out of touch with reality' but imaginative, the German replied.

The project would be linked to another free trade agreement, a Kaliningrad project like Mariupol. This lonely and embittered northern zone—the birth and deathplace of Immanuel Kant, lest we forget—also needs a Marshall Plan and liberation from the EU's stifling Customs border. It too requires a NEW CASABLANCA. In the treatise this 'multi-sided project' was referred to as a *triple project*.

- A rather improbable project.

- But interesting to more than one side and enjoying the oligarchs' support.

- How is this supposed to be pushed through with things as they stand at present?

- Obviously, it's not about enforcement, but project planning.

The intelligence officers conducting this conversation were sitting comfortably in the warmth of the wood-panelled bar. The assumption was that the 'doctoral student' had already made twelve trips by plane and two in rented yachts between Alexandria, Istanbul and Tel Aviv, not to mention a few cross-country ones, too.

Apparently, the thread of conversation had never been interrupted. Not all of them could be intercepted. Financing for the research trip, based on surprising gaps in reality, seemed stable.

- The company's financing is probably the only realistic thing about it.

- The travel costs seem to be covered.

- Absurd.

- And you think the young kid's ambition is to outperform his father?

- That seems to be what's driving him.

The more they reminded each other of the young adventurer's line of negotiation, the more the interlocutors came to like the theory that, in a hopeless situation, ANTI-REALISM and MAGNANIM-ITY ('generosity') alone could work wonders—just like at the pot-latch festival, a festival of abundance, among the Indians on the northwest coast of North America. From their schooldays, both were familiar with the example of a 'tug of war'. When one side unexpectedly lets go of the contested rope, the other side falls over.

The students who let go of the rope in time, the Briton added, have to help their opponents up immediately. They have to share their 'victory' with the other side.

- That would be unusual on a schoolyard.

FIGURE 21

FIGURE 22

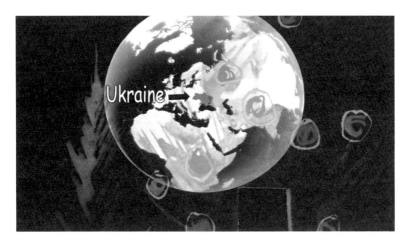

FIGURE 23

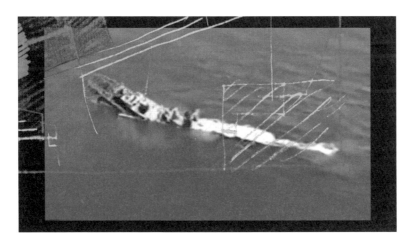

FIGURE 24. Sinking of the *Moskwa*.

STATION 4

'THE AMERICAN CIVIL WAR
IS NOT DEAD' /
WHAT DO WE KNOW ABOUT
THE UNFINISHED WARS
STILL RAGING BENEATH THE
GROUND OF OUR PLANET?

NEW WORLD, NEW WAR (1861–1865)

In the New World—as far as the Brothers Grimm could tell from afar, and the reason for the waves of immigration from Galicia, Ireland and Germany—everything is innovative, novel. More spacious, young, technical and overwhelmingly NEW.

That goes for war, too. In this case, the American Civil War. The industrialized north's stranglehold of the southern secessionists, renegades, slaveholders: 'Scott's Snake'. The secessionists, the Confederate States of America, who wanted to base their sovereignty on their own rights, who sought to separate themselves from the centre in Washington, were wracked by fears and anxieties. Fears are phantasmagorias, expectations are fantasies too: none of them are realistic. The southern states, once major players in American politics, expected to be overwhelmed, just as the waves of immigration had done in the north, by the creation of new states in the Midwest. They had never understood the North's Puritanism. They were afraid of a night of the long knives in the event of a rapid LIBERATION OF THE ENSLAVED, if, as in Saint Domingue, the ENSLAVED were to rise up violently against their former masters. Of course, there was also the arrogance of the South, a class society of glittering fortresses and homes, regionalism, nationalism and a rebellious spirit: a 'detached self-confidence' unattuned to the realities of the planet.

MOLE WAR

Wars unfinished continue to tunnel underground. They burrow onward through the centuries. Even trace elements from these tunnels can contaminate and ignite contemporary conflicts and are the explosives of our time.

A man from Minnesota who ended up at Harvard for a PhD (which is also where he is waiting for a planning position) has described in detail how the war in Ukraine that we are watching unfold without much influence on the belligerents arose from a kind of distant contamination. 'Things dream.' 'Wars dream.'

'THE THIN ICE OF CIVILIZATION'

As if descending from the US Capitol's oil paintings of the American Civil War, a REAL crowd of people, in costume, storm the seat of Congress on 6 January 2021. What is real? The pictures on the building's inner walls? The costumes? The spirits' unquiet? The unquiet between 1861–1865 or that of 2022? Or is only the SUM OF ALL PASTS, PRESENTS AND FUTURES real? Is an 'evil wind' unexpectedly blowing?

Blown by the Wind. Film triptych. 4 min 57 sec.

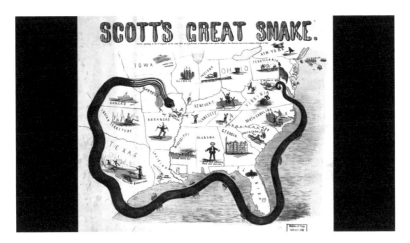

FIGURE 25. The strategic outline for overcoming the Confederate states envisaged the conquest of the Mississippi and the advance to New Orleans as the first stage of the war in the so-called *Western Theatre*. In the *Eastern Theatre*, in other words, the Atlantic coast, the Confederates' connection to Europe, to world trade and to all supplies was to be cut off by a blockade. In addition to sanctions. The author of the plan was named Scott. The project was known as SCOTT'S GREAT SNAKE (the Anaconda Plan).

Scott's Great Snake. Triptych. 6 min.

THE PERFECTLY SHAPED CAPITULATION
OF FORT APPOMATTOX

In the American Civil war, the Army of Northern Virginia, which had defended the capital of the Confederacy, capitulated at Appomattox. General Robert E. Lee, who signed the armistice, was a respected figure among the officials present, partly because of his teaching at West Point military academy before the outbreak of the war. His opposite, the commander-in-chief of the Union Army, also known as the Northern Army, was not the photographers' favourite subject. With his shoulder bag, he looked more like a 'wanderer' than a senior officer.

The capitulation was followed by a 'bad peace' with predatory confiscators. Northern tax collectors, adventurers, looters and indifferent and corrupt commanders of the occupying forces destroyed confidence in the capitulation agreements. Consternation among the defeated. For more than a hundred years after the war, the South felt impoverished and 'dispossessed'. This also applied to the 'liberated', that part of the population which had been delivered from slavery. In fact, some of the consequences of the war did not end until the arms boom of the Second World War, which, from 1944 onwards, drew workers from the southern states up to the northern industries in Chicago and Detroit.

FIGURE 26. General Lee, in grey, shakes the hand of General Grant, in blue, after signing the capitulation of his Army of Northern Virginia, which had been surrounded by the Union Army. Five days later, President Lincoln is assassinated in a loge at the theatre. This will remove a guarantee of fairness that the South has counted on.

'WAR DREAMS OF ABSOLUTE VIOLENCE'

FIGURE 27

FIGURE 28

FIGURE 29

FIGURE 30

FIGURE 31

FIGURE 32

FIGURE 33. The ancestors of today's HIMARS in Ukraine.
'Precision fire in 1864.'

FIGURE 34

FIGURE 35

STATION 5

FOG OF WAR

AN EXAMINATION TOPIC AT WEST POINT

The most feared final-exam topics at West Point had to do with the FOG OF WAR. This was Major General Freddy R. Williams' terrain, teacher of strategy and military historian. It does not have to do with troop deployment in sandstorms or in the fog, neither of which is a danger nor potentially disorienting to commander or troops any longer, as heat detectors possessed by orbiting scouts have made such opaqueness transparent; nor does the night hold any secrets for the satellite's eye, provided it involves living matter, which always gives off heat.

At the risk of appearing spiritual, Major General Williams put it this way: with the outbreak of war, the facts themselves lose their solid shape. Like animal combinations in Herodotus—according to which, for example, parts of a goat, a snake and a lion united to form an unknown animal known as the chimera—there were 'unknown facts' in war, mixtures of necessity and chance, which you could not prepare for through practice or toughening up. Indeed, it is not even certain that real conditions do not change minimally or 'bend' under the 'pressure-conditions of war', analogous to what happens to space and time in the immediate vicinity of monstrous gravitations. For the military-academy students, who had no experience of war, this was difficult to translate into an exam paper. To them it seemed 'philosophical in nature'. But this was precisely the kind of objection that Major General Williams vehemently rejected. The dangerous appearance of a 'degenerate reality' associated with so-called friction or the 'fog of war' was not of an intellectual nature whatsoever, i.e. it did not come from observation but from the things themselves. This is due to the 'warlike' contact of people and facts with chance. The leader of a military unit, like a ship sailing the open seas, gets caught up in the imponderables of chance which run rampant through the world. As soon as war breaks out, the facts can no longer be prevented from unauthorized contact with chance.

Was this just one of the Major General's obsessions? Or was it something that actually awaited the young officers in the future? Every year, the exam questions changed. The candidates took great care to try and learn all the solutions from the previous exams. They were convinced that these solutions could be copied, but that they could never find effective solutions to the fog of war itself. They were intimidated. But whenever Major General Williams got really excited in his seminars, he claimed that, like a 'wild hunt', the most turbulent spirits from all the wars of the past virtually conspired to push their way into the gaps that the facts always left between them. In this case, he argued, what provoked the facts to revolt wasn't any contact with chance at all, but with the 'dead generations of prehistory'. In any event, the Major General concluded, the result was the same: the fog of war was uncontrollable.

FOG OF WAR

'Everything in war is very simple,
but the simplest thing is difficult.
The difficulties accumulate
and end by producing a kind of friction.'

Carl von Clausewitz, *On War*[1]

DO NOT ATTACK IN FOG

On 12 February 1916, the day initially set to attack Verdun (everything was still undone), I drove to the front with two ordnance officers. Everything lay under an impenetrable layer of fog.

-   That can be an advantage. The defenders can't see a thing.

-   You mean that we should attack according to the compass? The squad doesn't have a compass.

-   You just have to charge straight ahead, always towards the west.

-   But we don't have any experience of attacking in fog. That has not been practised.

-   That's why I'm saying: this could be an advantage.

---

1 Carl von Clausewitz, *On War* (Michael Howard and Peter Paret trans.) (Princeton, NJ: Princeton University Press, 1976), BOOK 1, CHAP. 7.

The German supreme leadership, however, had been formed in the categories of 'clarity' and 'conscious resolution', that is, 'rationality'. They did not trust any 'more or less'.

- This is the day we were supposed to attack. We would have emerged from the mists like ghosts.

- And the artillery preparations? Were we just supposed to shoot blindly?

- You shoot according to maps anyway.

As I said, that day the order to attack was withdrawn. I stayed with the troops, crowded together in the tunnel where they lived and slept.

- And why do you assume the attack troops would have found their way?

- Because they would have run into the enemy.

- How are you supposed to recognize the enemy in the fog?

- Whoever's behind me is a friend. Whoever's in front of me is the enemy.

But in the fog, neither the 'in front of me' nor the 'behind me' could be made out with any certainty. Proceeding gropingly through the veils of fog, feet their only guidance, the soldiers tended to move in circles and confuse their directions, as became apparent on later occasions.

- It really could have turned into a mess.

- Yes, but a mess that could have been gradually steered to the west. We possessed magnesium flares. They would not have provided sight, but they would have provided signals.

'NERVES OF STEEL'

During the Battle of the Somme, officers from the Russia's Eastern Divisions were ordered to the Western Front under the assumption that they would react more calmly to the enemy's attacks, would perform their functions more 'objectively' in their command posts than those bundles of nerves who were commanding the Western Front. The fact that nerves could only tolerate stress up to a certain point and then fail was not functional: a 'howling wretch' was equally incapable of giving or carrying out orders. However, a 'howling wretch driven by the repressive function of an iron will' was non-functional too: just such an ego remained rigid and was unable to adapt orders or their execution to the concrete situation. The terrible thing, the officers freshly imported from the East (who were considered 'burnt out' after only a few weeks) reported, was not the enemy and his guns, but their own imagination, the one that accompanied orders to the troops. When we officers hold our men in the positions up front, we are considered executioners. Those who did not possess this imaginative faculty remained untroubled by the failure of their nerves. This type of unimaginative officer was useless in the war of movement. The keyword was: 'nerves of steel'. The search was on to find a way to install such a thing in the teams and officers. The military doctor, Dr Dänicke (professor ordinarius for neurology in Jena), said:

> Nerves do not have functions that are in any way reminiscent of steel. When two economies, i.e. industries, wrestle, and the side that endures longer than the other is eventually the winner, a feat is demanded of humans for which evolution has not prepared them: 'waiting under hopeless conditions'.

They tried it with 'butter cakes', so to speak, with a greasing of the nerves, if limited to official circles. 'Anaesthesia,' Dr Dänicke replied, 'or forced sleep, would be better.' Every case of an actual insertion of impulse lines of copper amalgam for experimental purposes to make the most severely wounded 'nerveless' led to the test subjects' deaths. The best remedy continued to be moving the men far to the back and prohibiting officers from visiting the front. That way at least the starting point of the order would remain intact.

The Demolition Expert of Vauquois.

THOSE HOLES IN THE HILLS OF VAUQUOIS

Beneath the village of Vauquois (which ceased to exist after the battle and which has not been rebuilt to this day) German and French pioneers, old-school mountain men, drove tunnels into the hill from both sides, reaching a depth of 60 metres and, as measured after the war, covering a combined distance of 17 kilometres. The blasting began with 50 kilograms of dynamite. Now, on 14 May 1916, one German charge had the destructive power of 60,000 kilograms of explosives. With it, the German miners blew up a slightly higher tunnel that belonged to the French miners who would otherwise have blown up the German tunnel. Inflation of resources in a very confined space.

–   Professionals, all of them.

–   Rapid loss rate of irreplaceable blasters and miners. They could not be pulled out as quickly as they perished.

–   On both sides of the hill, there were shelters and camps, not unlike a city, with depots, latrines, washrooms, kitchens . . . a barracks to feed the attack.

–   Ultimately, the hill became unusable for the construction of further tunnels. You can no longer build tunnels in earth that has been shaken by blasting.

–   What did the pioneers do then?

–   They built concrete pipes into the mountain.

–   Could you use them to blast?

–   The charge had to be increased again.

On the outside, it looked like cooperation. The concentrated labourers on both sides answered each other precisely. Never again was such skilled labour expended in such a confined space.

THE BATTLE FOR THE CARPATHIAN PASSES

Everything pointless. They did not arrive at the height of the Carpathian passes. The pass lay on one side near Radocyna, on the other near Konieczna. The Russian soldiers were wearing sleeping bags rolled up around their stomachs and backs. They worked their way up through the deep snow. Under fire from Schwarzlose and Maxim machine guns. Whenever a piece of a body was shot through, in that cold, there was no rescue. This also applied to the countesses, barons and bourgeois enthusiasts who, as officers, were driving these troops over the mountainside. To the side of the column, in front of the fire of the K.u.K. army, covered by a hill, a group of cameras had been set up on a wooden platform. They photographed the procession of the unfortunates trying to climb the pass. Even when they reached the top, these people would not have seen anything of their targets, the capitals of Budapest and Vienna. They would only have seen the masses of snow drifting down the slope.

Later, onscreen, they looked more like shadows than 'armed people'. From a distance, the shouldered, bayonetted carbines could have been sticks carried at random by the column, which kept moving away from the shelling to the side to protect itself in the snowdrifts. As the camera team only filmed the advance but not the late-afternoon retreat, a downhill flood to the northeast, the soldiers were heading for the uncertain passes for all eternity—as long as these propaganda films are shown in cinemas, that is. Always in vain. There was no question of a 'battle', as the inscriptions on the film canisters said. Some shot relentlessly from concealed positions in the air, others tried to dodge the bullets as best they could and, on this day at least, to get a few metres closer to the target—not to achieve that particular goal, but to bring the torture to an end.

IN THE PRISON OF DUTY

The German Supreme Army Command (OHL) did not issue any more orders in the Battle of Reims—the last offensive of the Reich in 1918—on the evening of 18 July. That meant a new dimension of despair. Was it the behaviour of players who had lost? No, it was the desperation of prison inmates: inmates in the prison of duty.

What does 'fulfilment of duty' mean? The paying off of a debt from a previous action? Senseless action? Endurance? Impossible to determine under conditions of despair. Someone who knew how to read the 1:300:000 maps and put them together could see the disaster. They talked about it with their companions, but nothing became any easier. Only this one doubt consisted of a complete picture. Losses, like the ones of that terrible day, could never be replaced. Dead, wounded, defectors—whole units were defecting to the enemy.

Similarly, the officers ran from room to room in the long corridors of Supreme Army Command. They were ashamed of one another. For months they had felt like they were PRISONERS OF DESTINY. The depression spread. Hardly anyone travelled to Berlin without leaving a piece of this PRISON OF PSYCHOSIS as a souvenir in the Reichstag or in the ministries; it was the army leadership that unnerved the political leaders at home.

How do you manage to find a WAY OUT OF SUCH SELF-INFLICTED DISCOURAGEMENT? Is there a WAY TO FREEDOM? Freedom would be a gun, von Lossow said. 'A shot through the temple.' They knew how to conquer foreign provinces. They didn't know how to find their way out of the prison of these STAFF QUARTERS OF A WAR GONE WRONG.

It wasn't a question of individual liberation, e.g. a fight, a night with the bottle. No, those days nobody was drinking. They knew that alcohol could lead to certain decisions: the deployment of regiments against their better judgement, suicide. Some would have liked to start drinking just to be able to sleep. How do you FIND YOUR WAY OUT OF SUCH CALAMITY, such bondage? Nothing can bring it about.

That day they abstained from all orders. Not every order had to consist of a phrase. That they had regretted their previous actions for four years already (or, when including preparation for the present crisis, even 16 or 20 years depending on how long they had served on the general staff) and that they would have liked to ask for forgiveness from those fighting and those who had fallen, that would have been a statement, not an order.

And so that evening there was no issuing of orders. At present, there is no PATH OF ENLIGHTENMENT. At the beginning of a military defeat based on past pride. No one can overcome this mountain of arrogance by walking backwards. Nor, beyond this arrogance, is there any WAY OUT TO THE COUNTRY THAT DOESN'T OPPRESS either.

KEYWORD: PARADOX

In ancient Greece, the adjective *parádoxos* meant: 'contrary to expectation', 'marvellous', 'self-contradictory'. A paradox is a contradiction that refuses our overarching understanding. Paradoxes cannot be mastered by humankind.

War is a demon that escapes the domination of those who instigate it as well as the desires of those who fight it. WAR IS A MASTER OF PARADOXES. This sentence by Herfried Münkler about the great war of 1914 to 1918 can be generalized. There is hardly a greater challenge to people's sensuality and intellect, to concept and view, to THEORY and POETRY, than WAR. It turns things on their heads and requires us to reorganize them. I would never have thought that, after the experiences in Central Europe in 1945 and 1918, it would be necessary to start thinking again.

WAR HAS NO SUPERIORS

WAR IS AN AMPHIBIOUS CONCEPT,
WHICH VACILLATES BETWEEN
ABSTRACTION AND CONCRETION

Immediately before Russia's attack on Ukraine in late February 2022, in a newspaper article, historian Herfried Münkler argued that the analogy to the Ukraine conflict was not to be sought in 1938 and 1939 but in the summer of 1914. Münkler describes the situation in that summer as follows:

'Two alliance systems, neither of which wanted the Great War, were heading for it due to a geopolitically subordinate issue. Neither side was prepared to lose face. Above all, neither wanted to risk the cohesion of the alliance to which it belonged, which could not be ruled out if it gave in. The question of the allies' reliability was at stake.'

To invoke military means only, the power of economic sanctions as opposed to armoured attack, questions of interest or legality (who promised something when in accordance with international law, who is committing war crimes?) is insufficient in such a situation. Rather, it concerns a kind of SECOND NATURE, holding together fragile alliances. It has to do with a LEVEL OF ABSTRACTIONS and writing, where language rules, agreements and common values are recorded. What triggers flight and causes death after the outbreak of war, that is, concretion, is a different aggregate state than 'political cartography'.

TAKING THINGS OVER

On 8 May 1916, an accident in the village of Douaumont. Flame-throwers leaking oil. The source of the flame cannot be extinguished. Ammunition dumps explode. The tunnels and halls of this concrete fortress storing everything that should be kept out of enemy fire for the time being. Columns flee through the corridors, 'a confused, psychologically infectious mass'. Those pushing forward do not give way to those fleeing from cross-corridors. Hand grenades are thrown.

As far as propaganda was concerned, Douaumont was a fortress in German hands. In reality, however, the concrete block was a junk room. The French had no weapons. And none of the fort's guns could be directed towards them. Thus it was merely a container for storing war materials.

These had now taken on a life of their own and were chasing the people out. If a commander had been available, at that moment, panic-stricken himself, he would have ordered the mountain to be cleared.

As the Commander-in-Chief's orderly officer, I get around a lot. It was quiet on the floor where I was. We were uneasy because we knew about the flames. Such fires only make a roaring sound right before they reach a room. Before that, they spread 'imperceptibly', they 'creep' (via electrical wires and concealed pipes). We felt defeated. We closed the double iron doors, taped all the sockets, checked that there were no heating pipes or supply lines leading to our shelter.

As an unconditional follower of Nietzsche, I am a good observer, especially in extreme cases. I tried to remain calm. I felt the ground and the walls shake from the explosions. Where is our WILLPOWER, our WILL, during such an event? That is what, *above all*, makes consciousness (which, among the occupants of the Douaumont, had obviously been thrown into turmoil and was confusing the senses) constitute the 'inner line of action', that is, the attitude that decides who wins and who loses. Were we simply lost or indeed losers? In the exact manner of observation of my master, I could only discover the WILL, i.e. the driving force of the event, in the flames themselves: in the flame-throwers (as we learnt later after reconstructing the event), namely, the first ones to explode and, in turn, awaken further explosions. For their part, these flame-throwers came from inventors and designers who had arranged these chemical warfare machines in such a way that they were suitable for 'smoking out' enemy bunker crews, but then, naturally, for destroying us, their triggers, too. It was a concentrate of HUMAN / EXTRA-HUMAN WILL: fire-breathing sticks, a flammable spray in our packs, a form of TOTAL WILL put together by chemically experienced *übermenschen*. It had exploded, fallen upon us, though, if I may be exact, such a piece of debris did not hit me, the philosophical observer.

–   A victory of things?

–   If you want to call the wall of flames that travelled through the tunnels a 'thing'. No one could have touched such a thing. It wasn't so much a thing as 'the will of its makers'.

–   The will of chance? 'The tool' escaping its 'guardians' and triggering a kind of slave revolt of things?

–   The slaves were those who'd been crammed into the concrete shafts. They had lost control of their senses as well as their minds. You cannot call what they were trying to save 'life'. How could they ever develop consciousness of themselves?

It seemed like a prophecy. What emerged here as a WILL TO POWER consisted of a complex prehistory and numerous reciprocities. In practice, the French arms industry's weapons lit our flamethrowers on fire, because one would never have existed without the other. The reign of things: a prophecy with no recipient as the matter was kept secret.

ASPEN IN SUMMER

If only there could be a hundred years of summers like this! The guests at the conference were spellbound by the exhilaration of being part of the chosen few. What is the average opinion of 87 people, all of whom are determined not to say anything that might upset the others, nothing at all displeasing so that they would not be invited back? As far as China was concerned, the US was still able to move freely thank to its maritime monopoly. But what will happen in 40 years? The theme of the conference was: Agenda 2040.

– They think incessantly about the right time to solve the Taiwan problem once and for all by simply wiping it off the table.

– Who exactly are you referring to?

– China's military planners.

At that time, Danish intelligence had the best information about the state of consultation in the Chinese military leadership. Without having done much, the Danes had managed to have a mole at the core of China's leadership. Now, the small NATO partner possessed an excessive amount of information, which it discreetly shared with the US. According to that information, in Chinese military doctrine, a blitzkrieg (as Japan had waged in 1941, Germany had planned in 1914 and MacArthur had failed to achieve in Korea in 1951) was considered objectionable. No one whose career was important to them would ever suggest invading an island to the Central Committee if they did not know what options China might have in the ensuing conflict. They have ostracized all 'adventurers' in their ranks, the informant reported.

– What do you understand by 'wiping it off the table'?

– Why?

- You were speaking about Taiwan, Taiwan isn't on any kind of table.

- It's an expression.

- Realities are born of expressions.

- Comparing expressions and births is absurd.

The Danish expert, a major general, the mole's case officer, wanted to explain to his higher-ranking US counterpart that the Chinese leadership was by no means 'playing for time'. They aren't playing at all, he said. Nor is it 'keeping a low hegemonic profile to buy time and, later, suddenly assume the traits of a monster'. The faction in the US that was concerned with their 'future chief rival, China' at the time was too excited to pay attention to the news of the small NATO partner.

In an article for the *Journal of Foreign Affairs* the following day, that same US chief who left the Dane standing (only because Wolfowitz had just entered the conference room) wrote: 'With all the technological means available to a superpower in the twenty-first century, wars can still be triggered by assessing the situation incorrectly.' This was currently aimed at Iraq and was a barb towards the predominant *net-centric-warfare* wing in the Pentagon which had taken over all planning positions and budgets. A successful bit of spite. The statement wasn't directed at the grey area of 2040, that point in time when the anti-China faction thought it would already have long been in power.

STATION 6

HUMAN NATURE AND
BITTER WAR /
IN AGGRESSION'S ZOO /
'THE ABILITY TO MOURN'

OUTBREAK OF WAR DUE TO DEPRESSIVE TYPES

Driving down a lane of his Hohenfinow estate in the autumn of 1913, Chancellor of the German Reich, Theobald von Bethmann Hollweg, who in July 1914 began his 'leap into the dark' which meant the outbreak of war, gave the following prophecy: 'Sooner or later, this avenue will be cut down by the Russians; for sooner or later they will flood this area. Most likely sooner rather than later. They are smothering us with their mass.'

Consequently, as soon as it was seen from a historical perspective, there was nothing more to save. Hollweg believed in the inevitability of world war. The idea paralysed him. But it would not be the Russians who would come first, 'smothering us with their mass'; no, 28 years later, German armoured divisions would enter Russia. In the fifth year of the war, however, this would indeed lead Russian armies as far as Hollweg's Hohenfinow lane. But the trees were not chopped down at that time either. 'The Chancellor expected a war, whatever the outcome, to overturn everything that existed.'![1]

---

1 Erdmann, on Bethmann Holweg, in *Geschichte und Unterricht* 9 (1964): 536. The dissertation of the close advisor to the Reich Chancellor, Kurt Riezler, bears the title *The Necessity of the Impossible: Prolegomena to a Theory of Politics and Other Theories* (1913). The book is a polemic against Bismarck's coinage 'politics as the art of the possible'. Bismarck's perspective, the impatient and depressed of 1914 said, did not lead to any horizons.

OUTBREAK OF WAR DUE TO AGGRESSIVE TYPES

Aggressive, that is, hostile, willing to attack, irritable, always direct and ready to use violence, that was the president of the USA, George Walker Bush, Jr. Nevertheless, the war against Iraq and the attack on Afghanistan were not just a result of his temperament. These had been prepared by aggressive lobbyists and Republican-minded scientists in the foundations of Washington. It was there in the foundations and think tanks that the plans for the defeat of Islam, the defeat of Iran, a GENERAL SOLUTION IN THE MIDDLE EAST emerged. Logic, geopolitics, overarching planning are aggressive mobiles of the mind. What brings about attacks is not an individual, but organized mind.

The initiator of the erroneously calculated war of aggression against Ukraine, President Putin, is described by an employee in the Federal Chancellery, who is also responsible for briefing the chancellor, as 'DEFENSIVE-AGGRESSIVE'. Putin, as befitting his origins, is a street fighter from St Petersburg. He reacts aggressively to every violation of his circle, as he once did to other street gangs. If the borderline is violated, the neighbourhood he defends, or his mother—a concierge he protects—he will strike back. In that sense, he is aggressive. However, he has no tendency to go beyond 'defending with aggressive means'. The expert is of the opinion—and writes it into the sketches he prepares for the chancellor—that, despite randomly picked occasional remarks, one should not ascribe to him any fantastic expansionist fantasies.

What would or could he gain by subjugating recalcitrant Balts or Poles? ANOTHER COLLEAGUE IN THE FEDERAL CHAN-CELLERY WHO IS ALSO RESPONSIBLE FOR BRIEFING THE CHANCELLOR VEHEMENTLY DISAGREES. The secret-service studies do not provide any evidence for either one or other of these hypotheses.

BIODIVERSITY OF AGGRESSION

Whether Genghis Kahn and the Mongol rulers who advanced westwards after his death were aggressive or acted on psychic programmes alien to us or were afflicted by EXTRA-TERRESTRIAL SOULS on a pilgrimage on earth remains unexplored. In any event, little of Mongolia's riches are present in today's People's Republic of Mongolia.

Immediately after 1918, an equestrian general of the Tsar, a Baltic baron named von Ungern-Sternberg, generally considered an aggressive character, founded a Mongolian Equestrian Division and, as an alleged descendant of Genghis Khan, declared parts of the 'Roof of the World' as his empire while endeavouring to extend his sphere of influence to Europe. His plan was to militarily capture the express-train line from Riga to Paris, and travel to France with his squadrons harnessed to horses in special wagons. Intercepted by Red Army units far from Riga, he was killed by firing squad.

A hymnic work by Voltaire is about Charles XII of Sweden. The philosopher was enchanted by the aggressive spirit of this descendant of King Gustav Adolf. Charles XII advanced far into Russia with his small, disciplined army. He added victory to victory. Until, at Poltava in Ukraine, Tsar Peter struck him on the head. The Swedish king fled into a long exile in the Orient.

An oligarch has built a 'zoo of aggressiveness' in the immediate vicinity of the huge new spaceport on the Amur River, where the Russian Space Agency moved from Baikonur in Kazakhstan. He believes that the biodiversity of aggressiveness on earth is under threat by waves of moralization. The idea behind his zoo is that there are not just a few but a few thousand types of aggression, some of which are necessary to combat more dangerous types of aggression. The full score of all aggressions, as in mathematics a minus multiplied by a minus becomes a plus, is not a trigger for war. This zoo founder explains his project by saying that we need ARTISTE DÉMOLISSEURS, 'destruction artists', to break through those realities that produce war and to reach deep down into the character of human beings to the CURRENT OF EQUALITY that he believes flows through millions of years of evolution as well as through the 8 billion people living today.

GENEROSITY AS AN EMPIRE'S FOUNDATIONAL MYTH

The ALEXANDER ROMANCE tells the story of Alexander the Great some 1,500 years after his death. The Grand Dukes of Burgundy had chosen this Macedonian king to be their idol and had his deeds woven into tapestries. This Alexander conquered the Persian Empire. If he hadn't died, he would probably have linked the rest of the world in the west (as far as Gibraltar) with his conquests in the east, which reached as far as the Indus.

Historian Alexander Demandt does not consider this conquering king to have been aggressive, even if often victorious. Between his battle at Issus and the battle at Gaugamela, which subdued the Persian Empire, he took two years to found cities, gain experience, spread education, visit temples and oracles, places of knowledge. His wars are the only example, according to Demandt, of a war of aggression that produced a long-lasting result, namely, Hellenic antiquity.

Alexander was considered irascible and generally quick-tempered. But in a second soul he was of resolute patience, a man full of GENEROSITY. He generously distributed Persia's gold reserves, buried in the treasure house of the great kings, around the world. This brought about an economic rise and the miracle of fortune and spirit that was Hellenism, which lasted 300 years.

He celebrated one of his victories with a collective wedding feast of a thousand of his warriors with a thousand women from the conquered empire, as if to transport the war to the horizons. Other foundations of lasting empires through war are unknown.

THE FATALISM OF FORESIGHT AND FANTASIES
AS GROUNDS FOR WAR

Children lie. I lied as a child to avoid punishment. They said: 'He who lies steals and later beats people to death.' This did not happen with me.

In the 1930s, which Florian Illies reflects in his book *Love in a Time of Hate* (people's SUBJECTIVE SIDE lies less than history), the so-called YELLOW PERIL was a public issue. In a science-fiction novel by Hans Dominik, huge air fleets, warlike zeppelins, airborne platforms ('rafts of air') with artillery, fantastic types of flying machines from the Far East and from a fantasized China as well as from a mysterious 'Roof of the World' fly aggressively towards Europe.

It is not impossible that ancestral FANTASIES like this one are playing out in the West's current perception of existing provocations from a NEW CHINA.

Heiner Müller points out that there is no mental authority that sorts between factual perception and the currents of the imagination. Between good and evil, a load of literature and oversight. Between the fantastic and the real: free trade.

DEALING WITH AGGRESSIVE, REVISIONIST POWERS / HOW DOES ONE REPLY TO AGGRESSIVE REVISIONISM?

Historian Herfried Münkler describes those few cases in which a longer lasting peace agreement was reached. He mentions the end of the Thirty Years' War in the Peace of Münster and Osnabrück (the result of a negotiation process that lasted five years), the Congress of Vienna of 1815 (which ended the Napoleonic Wars without igniting a spirit of revenge in defeated France). He also refers to a report by Henry Kissinger on the cooperation of Egypt's President Sadat in trying to end the Yom Kippur War. In addition, Münkler cites the Marshall Plan and the international economic integration of German reconstruction after 1945 as a successful operation that precluded new German revisionism.

All other attempts to distract a revisionist power from war or to dissolve the revisionist motive through appeasement, economic incentives or deterrence have failed due to half-heartedness. Indifference to the vanquished and a failure to perceive their vulnerability were just as aggressive as the aggressiveness lurking within them.

ON THE KEYWORD *REVISIONIST*

The Yugoslav Wars, also known as the post-Yugoslav wars of dis-integration, were based on a chain of previous unresolved conflicts. The disintegration of Austria-Hungary and the Ottoman Empire left behind arbitrary borders. 'ETHNIC, MENTAL, HISTORIC, ECONOMIC TANGLES' emerged—no inherently coherent polities in themselves and thus full of outwardly directed expectations, intent on gain. This need not have led to the Yugoslav Wars, wars that have existed since the liberation of the Balkans from Ottoman rule. Revisionist aggression requires, in addition to the perception of one's own uniqueness, an imaginative narrative. It is what underlies all radical nationalism. REVISIONIST AGGRESSION is what demands a change or defence of national borders as if it were a matter of one's own skin. It is not an authentic expression of human beings' nature. Rather, it is a form of civilizational, highly complex 'abstract' agitation rooted in the so-called superego. If an individual is in immediate distress, alone or tired, this strong driving force disintegrates. It is an 'unnatural force of the soul'.

'THE SKIN KNOWS WHEN
WARS ARE GOING TO END
BEFORE THE HEAD'

Sigmund Freud considered both public moral opinion as well as parts of our power of reason, which he attributed to the psychic instance of the so-called superego, to be the EXTENDERS and INITIATORS OF WAR.

What is reliably anti-war, or at least a reliably anti-military element, he says, is the skin. In humans, it is the largest organ in terms of surface area. This was written in a 1939 letter to Albert Einstein, the physicist whom he implicitly accused of not taking sufficient account of the human soul in his view of the world. What Freud had in mind were the drenched bodies of Galician recruits in the caves and caverns of the Alpine war of 1917—as Freud had never been involved in warfare himself. Wet to the skin, their skin froze. For months, these 'skin owners' could not wash. Their uniforms were sticky. On the opposite front, the war machine had transported soldiers from Puglia and Calabria to that icy zone in the Alps. There, in a terrestrial moonscape, they lay facing the 'enemy', without any warlike motives of their own, just as drenched, freezing, disturbed by fungi and parasites, 'up close and personal with their own skin'. The skin did not obey any command of the ego, the superego, the unconscious or 'social command'. The rocks at the soldiers' backs and the field gendarmerie on all the passes prevented them, on both sides, from escaping.

Your own skin responds confidently to a situation 'without an emergency exit'. It reddens, becomes inflamed. According to Freud, a SKIN ALLERGY corresponds to a *levée en masse* in a revolutionary society. Eventually, the soldier can no longer endure a uniform (his social skin) on his body. He throws off the mask in terms of his face and posture too. Not of his own free will, but due to the general strike in his body, represented by his skin. Everything that made him a suitable tool of war collapses long before the war itself becomes insolvent. The war ends because the combatants can no longer do anything, regardless of what they may want, and regardless of the possession of this will by the leaders throughout the general staffs. 'Anti-colonialism of the will'. The skin defends itself over every head. We say: 'I'm defending my skin.' But even this impulse is refuted by the skin itself, which says: 'I am no longer prepared to even fight back.' The 'logics of war' are inflationary. Only the 'anti-logic' of the naked skin is solid. It has black market chains, tunnels and channels to the nerves far below the 'domineering brain'.

ANECDOTE

During a brief standstill in the middle of the battle in the Hundred Years' War between France and England, a group of 50 French prisoners waited to be massacred. These were people from whom no ransom could be expected. Freed by a French counterattack in the still-undecided battle, they would be a danger to the British. And so, in the next few minutes, they were to be murdered.

Then, all of a sudden, a random cloud, a hellish thunderstorm with heavy rain and lightning interrupted the logic of the event. The rain poured into the English henchmen's armour, and the executors, summoned for an immediate execution, became soaked to the skin. Nothing could dry or wipe away the wetness. It was virtually impossible to open the suits of armour when the leather straps were soaked. The desperate guards (and future executioners) built a fire. They prepared a meal, got drunk to ease the torment. Exhausted by the weather, the wet and the wait, they fell asleep. The prisoners escaped.

The random clouds of 'heavy rain', the random clouds of the as-yet-'undecided battle', the random clouds of the 'forces of mind, i.e. the fighters' subjective side' show little connection logically or in accordance with their backgrounds. The gaps in the logic were enough to act as an emergency exit for the rescued prisoners. Logic itself would have killed them.

A QUIP FROM KARL MARX
DURING THE CRIMEAN WAR (1853–1856),
SHARED AT A SALON

–   Which animal would you compare the demon of war to? A snake?

–   Perhaps a hydra.

–   That would be more than one thousand snakes' heads. Each with venomous teeth.

–   No one has seen ever a hydra. Or, I haven't, in any event.

–   But possible as a metaphor.

–   Depictable by means of letters? Or in music?

–   Many attempts in the visual arts have been in vain. Dürer's thundering *Horsemen of Apocalypse* only roughly reflect the reality of war. War is no horseman, nor 'trinity', and with its treacherous creeps and PHANTASMAGORIA, its chameleon-like transformations and PERSISTENCE (as far as its return is concerned) is incomparable to anything in painting.

–   Is war mathematical?

–   Few parts of it. It is as if one had closed an eye, and with the second saw a demon that behaved 'anti-mathematically'.

–   And 'seeing' would be an exaggeration?

–   One cannot see war.

–   With what senses, what human powers of mind could one deal with war?

–   What do you mean by 'deal with'? Observe it? Get to the bottom of it? End it? 'Overwinter' it? 'Forget'? 'Fritter away'? 'Oversleep'? 'Sabotage' it?

–   The sum of all those would be something good.

THE OPPOSITE OF WAR IS NOT 'PEACE' BUT 'ANTI-WAR': A CONTINUAL PROCESS, WHICH IS BEST TO BEGIN IN THE MIDDLE OF WAR

– For the search term ANTI-WAR, one needs, unusually in col-
   loquial language, all the senses, the five natural senses (above
   all, their derivatives and extensions), the 32 'social senses', the
   collective sense that knows how to sail the clouds of causality,
   CURIOSITY FOR THE UNEXPECTED AND THE UTTERLY
   IMPLAUSIBLE, the senses that direct their sensors into the
   future, the future that still wants to be born, the roots at work
   in the past: a cosmos of desires, senses, search terms, stories
   and springs.

– Don't you think that you are mixing the various forms of reality
   here?

– No reality without diversity.

– Would that be a 'spirit in all things'?

– You mean a fantasy?

– When reality becomes deadly, a fantasy; if it opens an emergency exit, it is nothing unrealistic.

– Once again: What is a war that doesn't want to die? It has the
   aftertaste of the uncanny. As if it were accompanying humankind like a shadow. It gives the appearance of being powerful
   in reality . . .

The philosopher Moellendorff from Marburg, a scholar from the
USA, with whom this conversation took place, considered war a
fantasy and not an inevitability. He denied it LOGIC. So far, he
claims, all wars have died, some downright extinct. In evolutionary
terms, war cannot present itself as a 'victorious power' anywhere.

– It kills, but remains a dreamer . . .

– In relation to itself as a decision maker.

Humanity's accessory kit, the obstetrician of nothing, replied Moellendorff. The conversation, which lasted until four o'clock in the morning as both dialogue partners felt emotionally engaged, preferring to work on an infinite melody rather than sleep, two obsessives, so to speak, splintered apart. The demon of war was gifted in terms of technical inventions, but not in terms of a vaccination against itself. At the same time, it was certainly mortal. Different from the people it killed, but just as finite. The dialogue partners agreed. In that late hour, the two came to the understanding, without noting it, that above all during and under the immediate effects of INSANE WARS the chance to investigate remedies against repetitions of the respective insanities—they are especially hidden in subterranean rivers—exists. This is best done neither in the pre-war nor in the postwar, but in the current war—*ex bello*. Before the war, after the war, the sensual and conceptual forces are not sufficient for anything that could reliably sabotage the new formation of causes of war, just as the body's resistance forces only counteract infection during illness. In the year 2022, humanity had nothing more to offer for a PERSPECTIVE OF HAPPINESS than this NIGHT OF TWO ENLIGHTENED SPIRITS.

'THERE IS A REASON
BEHIND EVERY ERROR'

There is a reason behind every error.
The search for reasons digs up and
finds a treasure trove of experiences.
There is more experience in the reasons
that lead to error than in the
collections of true propositions.

KING CROESUS' ERRORS

King Croesus, a ruler of Asia Minor, thought he was a lucky man. To improve his luck, however, he bribed the oracle. The oracle took revenge by giving him ambiguous information. Croesus had asked whether he should wage war against the Great King of Persia. The oracle had answered: 'If you cross the border river, you will destroy a great empire.' Croesus assumed that this meant Persia. In fact, he was doubly mistaken: he lost the war, and his own empire was destroyed. In the end, he stood at the stake to await his death. But the fundamental error was that a ruler who starts a war can somehow determine it. Once war has broken out, the ruler ceases to rule. 'War tolerates no superiors.'

> Modernism ignited within an aggressive milieu.
> It emerged from the seriousness of war. The seriousness of war is the father of the end of war.

FILMS

Dynamite Tango. With Sir Henry.
1 min 6 sec.

The Woman on the Battlefield.
1 min.

Battle of the Marne Tango.
2 min.

Colonel Bruchmüller.
5 min 2 sec.

Time After the Downfall. 39 sec.

FIGURE 36. László Moholy-Nagy of the *Bauhaus*
(*Me as Wounded Man*, c.1917), 2019.
Painted after the original by Ivan Syros, 2019.

THE EMERGENCE OF THE MODERN
OUT OF THE SPIRIT OF HOWITZER ORDNANCE MAPS

In the third year of the First World War, the 'disruption of all circumstances', the unwillingness to end pointless battles, caused a minority of officers to doubt the 'role of artillery in a strategy of annihilation'. It virtually trapped the enemy in the trenches of positional warfare instead of driving them away. There was a weariness with the artillery's acquired, rehearsed, 'managed work of annihilation': an 'allergy of the mind'. In Italy and Germany, the idea of the 'stormtrooper' was born.

Colonel Bruchmüller, a reformer of the artillery, retired, is called back to service. Over the course of 1917, the 'destructive fire' that had characterized the battle of Verdun was replaced by the 'revolutionary tactics' of artillery which focused on pinpoint fire—that is, on target points such as road intersections, supply depots and enemy command centres—similar to the technology of HIMARS rocket artillery in Ukraine in 2022. This is the same spirit in which the engineer Robert Musil, Austrian officer in the Alpine War in 1917, sharpens his powers of observation. Until the end of his life, in 1942, in the middle of the Second World War, he drilled and dug into a textual edifice that began in 1913 and illuminated all sides of the sphinx-like modern age.

Franz Kafka joins in 1916. He wants to record the madness of his time in a novel about the retreat of the Napoleonic army in Russia in the winter of 1812. László Moholy-Nagy, who would later become an activist at the Bauhaus, was working on the measuring table data for heavy howitzers at the time of the war. From these roots, mathematics and the art of shooting, constructivism emerged after the war. As late as 1943 in Chicago, where the most powerful armament machine of the Second World War is being built, you can see BAUHAUS PEOPLE and MODERNISTS at work on the war. The theme is now camouflage. When the enemy develops the art of covering its factories with camouflage nets while erecting fake ones on nearby farmland, the artist, the 'aesthetic structuralist', can still see the shadows cast by the camouflaged buildings on the adjacent terrain. One of the oldest arts, that of Ulysses: cunning, masks, camouflage, disguise, uncovering the trick, etc., functions like an engine of modernity. The dialectic of enlightenment points forwards and far backwards in history.

The Emergence of the Modern out of Howitzer Ordnance Maps. 7 min.

A LIBIDINOUS REASON FOR OBJECTIVITY

Evolutionist Dr Erwin Boltzmann believes that the majority of all people who survived throughout history possessed a 'raw form of good will': an exuberant power that does not quite match any of its other 'useful' abilities. This 'special admixture' can be observed in the agricultural revolution of the last 7,000 years. That it is causal for reproduction, i.e. for direct offspring, cannot be proven.

Objectivity, in other words, third-party usability, Boltzmann says, is a derivative of Narcissus (who desired a relationship with his own image).

What would you call this millennial attraction for objectivity? Dr Boltzmann is asked. I repeat, Dr Boltzmann says, I call the libidinous reason for such objectivity: self-respect.

'THEY FIGHT, THEY FALL'
(HOMER)

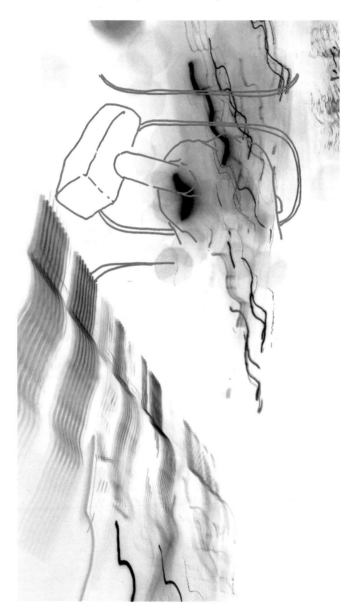

FIGURE 37

FIGURE 38

FIGURE 39

FIGURE 40

In 1932, the year I was born, there was an image of a dogfight (in other words, air-to-air combat) in an illustrated newspaper. 'If the armed passenger kills the pilot, they both will crash.' The masses of reality set in motion by a war are not solid ground. Rather, they have a drop height similar to that of a dogfight. At best, they are like the water in which the Titanic sank.

BISMARCK'S TEARS OVER AN UNWANTED VICTORY PARADE

When I think of the phrase 'making peace', my father, a doctor, told me, I see a man who was said to have 'iron hardness', Count Bismarck. He is not yet a prince, not yet Chancellor of the Reich. He is sitting in a twilit parlour in a castle south of Königgrätz. That was the name of the previous day's battlefield in the Prussian version. The Austrian army is defeated. This man, who is said to be somewhat petrified, is a 'moving and agitated spirit'. He feels 'responsible'. He 'weeps', tears streaming from both eyes. It is a salty liquid, originally derived from the organs of sea animals, the ancestors of Prussian nature, too. That was at least 5 million years ago. The ability to liquefy fossilized matter has been preserved from that long ago. To drive salt from the inside of soul and body to the outside.

The reason behind such tears: the King of Prussia insists on marching to Vienna after the victorious battle. There he wants to hold a VICTORY PARADE. From the gut upwards, Bismarck has an agitated physical life, and above it rises a soul that knows: if we triumph, we will prolong the war indefinitely.

He was unable to prevent future wars with his mourning work in the twilight hour. On 30 April 1945, his portrait was still hanging in the bunker of the Reich Chancellery where Hitler committed suicide. Then it is cut out of the frame, rolled up and smuggled through the Russian lines to the West. The portrait's presence in the Reich Chancellery did not prevent the outbreak of war in 1939. Now, however, in 1866, the 'great, tearfully distorted face', its openness, its lack of arms unsettles the king, his insistence on a parade. No parade, no continuation of the war. This is the art of healing. And yet, this Prussian aristocrat was no doctor.

WHAT STRENGTHENS THE EYE MORE, A TELESCOPE OR A TEAR?

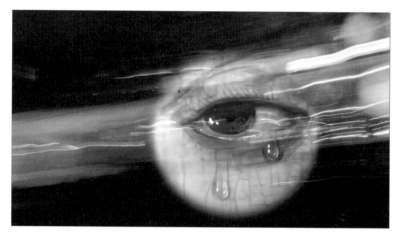

FIGURE 41. *The Impossibility of Not Crying.*
From the series 'Lights in the Harbour'. Aluminium print, 19 x 16.5 in.
Galerie Knust / Kunz Munich, 2022.

Here you have a tear. Behind it you see light from the port of Amsterdam. The ability to cry is something wonderful. It shows that we are descended from sea animals. Because they are the only beings which can transport salty liquid from the inside to the outside. This ability to turn something fossilized within me into liquid is the basis of all music. The core form of music is the *lamento*, the dirge.

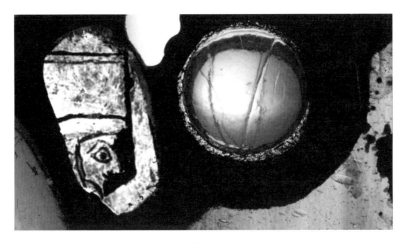

FIGURE 42

This is a glass panel. In the middle is a stone from Sigmar Polke. He collected stones like this. They remained in his estate. Which is from where Kerstin Brätsch removed it to place within a glass panel. I have placed in turn a section of the glass panel before my camera lens. Next to it is a 6,000-year-old picture from Uruk. The whole thing is a *constellation* and is based on the cooperation between a painter's collection, an artist's glass panels and my film work. At the same time, the resulting image continues the work of an unknown person from 6,000 years ago. That is what film can do. The art of film is young. It is particularly good at constellating and combining opposites.

> The ability to mourn. This is the point at which the liquid element and the stone within us—the stony heart—rub against each other.

IT MAY BE PREMATURE WHEN,

GIVEN MEN AS THEY ARE,

THE TREES SURRENDER . . .

NOTE

The epigraph to this book comes from poet Ben Lerner's *The Lichtenberg Figures*. Georg Christoph Lichtenberg's (1742–1799) oeuvre is one of the pearls of THE AGE OF ENLIGHTENMENT. Lichtenberg's *Figures* have to do with lightning, which he captured on glass plates.

I dedicate this little book to Ben Lerner.

Figures 2, 3, 4, 37, 39 and 40 are drawings by Thomas Thiede.

ACKNOWLEDGEMENTS

When I was a pupil, we learnt to read and write with a primer. When war breaks out, Bertolt Brecht said, we have to learn to read and write again. Something is wrong, we have to start over. For that we need fibulae, and fibulae should be short. I have never worked as closely with an editor as I did with Wolfgang Kaußen in shortening this text from 400 to 120 pages. I would also like to thank its producer Ute Fahlenbock and my colleagues Barbara Barnak and Gülsen Döhr.